The Wild Christmas Reindeer

written and illustrated by

JAN BRETT

PaperStar

The Putnam & Grosset Group

A PaperStar Book, published in 1998 by The Putnam & Grosset Group,
200 Madison Avenue, New York, NY 10016. PaperStar is a registered
trademark of The Putnam Berkley Group, Inc. The PaperStar logo is
a trademark of The Putnam Berkley Group, Inc.
Originally published in 1990 by G. P. Putnam's Sons.
Published simultaneously in Canada. Printed in the United States of America
Airbrush backgrounds by Joseph Hearne
Type design by Gunta Alexander
Library of Congress Cataloging-in-Publication Data
Brett, Jan. The wild Christmas reindeer /
written and illustrated by Jan Brett.   p.   cm.
Summary: After a few false starts, Teeka discovers the best way to get
Santa's reindeer ready for Christmas Eve.
[1. Reindeer—Fiction. 2. Christmas—Fiction.] I. Title.
PZ7.B7559Wi   1990   [E]—dc20   89-36095   CIP   AC
ISBN 0-698-11652-6
7   8   9   10

To
Natalie and Stephanie
Larsen

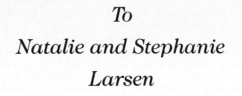

Teeka was excited. And a little afraid. This year Santa had asked her to get the reindeer ready to fly on Christmas Eve. Teeka had never done this before and she wanted everything to be perfect.

Teeka lived up in the Arctic in the shadow of Santa's Winter-farm. The last of the snow geese had flown south, and everyone's mind was on Christmas. The workshop was alive with the sounds of saws sawing, hammers hammering, and brushes painting as they all worked to have the toys and presents ready for delivery on Christmas Eve.

Teeka knew it was time for her to go in search of the reindeer.
They had been out on the tundra, wild and free since last
Christmas, and Teeka was sure they wouldn't want to go back to
Winterfarm to train. She would have to be strong and firm.

At last she found them. Bramble and Heather, Windswept and Lichen, Snowball, Crag, Twilight and Tundra.

Teeka took a deep breath and shouted out, "Let's go! Move, move, move!"

The reindeer were bewildered by Teeka's voice. Their heads went up to see who this loud creature was.

But they let her herd them together and headed back toward Winterfarm. Tundra gave her the most trouble. Teeka didn't know that he considered himself the leader and was not used to being bossed around. He liked to stay next to Twilight, but she was separated from him and running near the front. When they got to the barn, Teeka put them in different stalls. Tundra snorted impatiently.

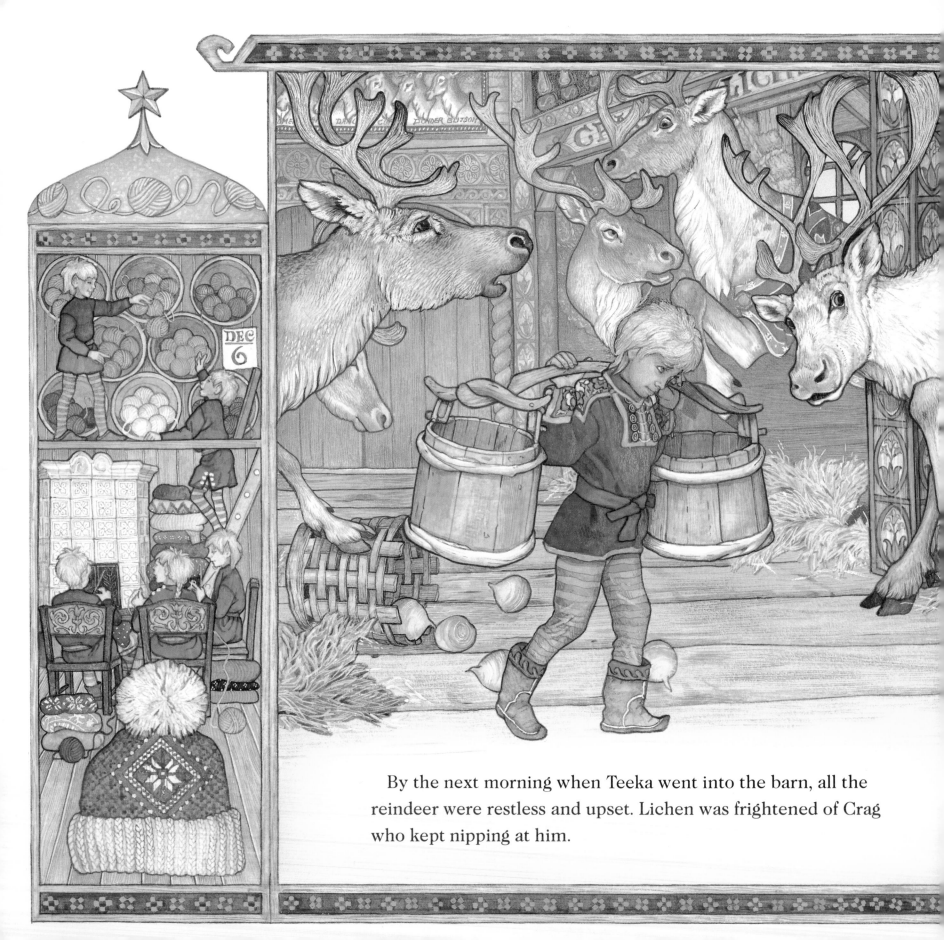

By the next morning when Teeka went into the barn, all the reindeer were restless and upset. Lichen was frightened of Crag who kept nipping at him.

Bramble was so worried, she drove Heather wild. And Twilight
kept calling out to Tundra who was just plain angry and stamping
his hooves.

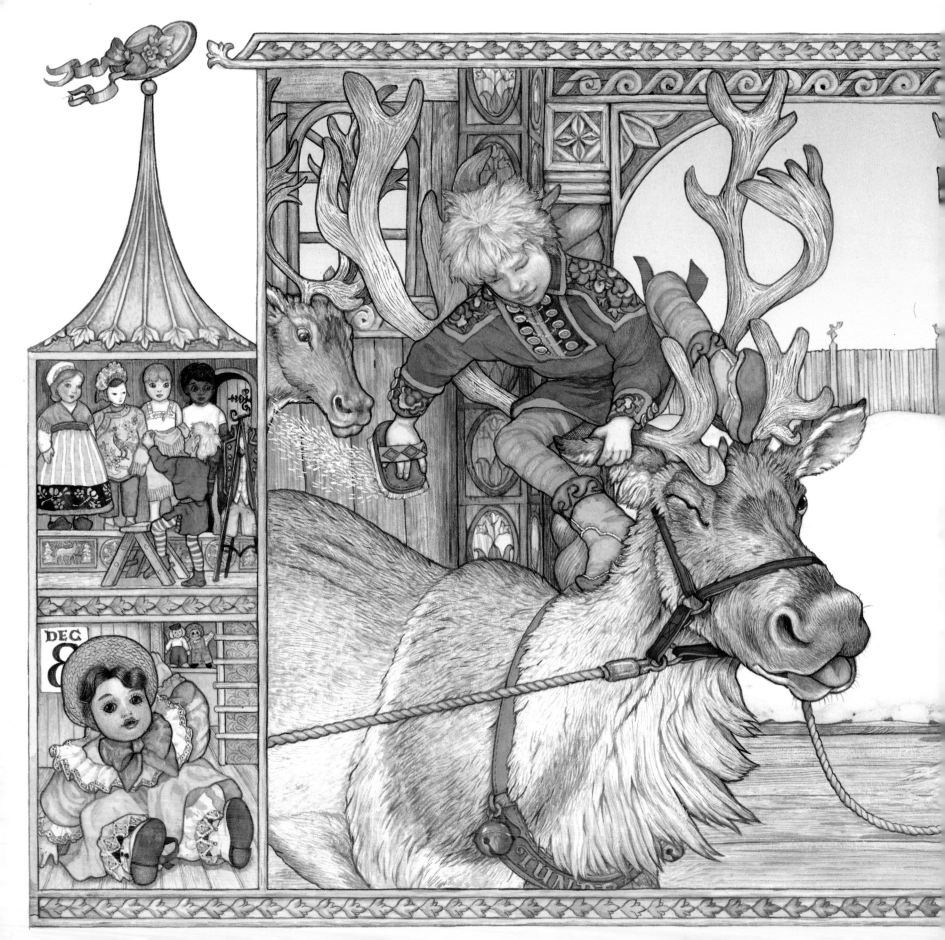

Teeka groomed each reindeer. She wanted them to look sleek
and glossy for Santa. One by one, she brushed and combed their
coats and pushed and pulled at their tangled manes. She brushed
so long and hard that their ears started to turn pink.

DEC
9

Teeka took the reindeer outside. Now she was ready for the real training to begin. Snowflakes danced in the air as she tried to stand them in two lines and put on their harnesses. But they wouldn't stay lined up. She had put Tundra at the back with Heather instead of at the front with Twilight, so he kicked out at Heather who then bolted into Bramble.

Teeka scolded the reindeer. "Don't move!" she cried. But they all ran off wild-eyed, and she had to go after them and bring them back.

The next day Teeka harnessed the reindeer in the barn before taking them out into the snow. Everything went right until she got them lined up outside and tried to steer them first to the left and then to the right. To make the sleigh fly, they would need to pull together smoothly. But everything went wrong.

Tundra crashed into Heather, Snowball blew up at Bramble.
Windswept knocked over Twilight. And then, Lichen locked
antlers with Crag.

"Stop!" Teeka cried, as she watched the reindeer paw the air. "Unhook!" she shouted, as they tried to free their long antlers.

Then Lichen and Crag fell over into the snow. The harder they pulled, the more their antlers locked. The reindeer were frantic and Teeka only made it worse by yelling at them.

Tundra and Heather rushed to help, but the antlers did not break free. Windswept nudged at Lichen, and Bramble ran to help Crag. But the more they tried to help, the more they got tangled up themselves. Their necks strained and their muscles bulged, but their antlers did not budge.

Teeka wailed, "Oh, please! It's almost Christmas Eve!"

But the reindeer could not move.

A frosty silence hung in the air.

Dec
17

Teeka looked at the tangled reindeer, once so bold and free, and began to cry. "It's my fault," she said. "I've spent all my time yelling at you, instead of helping. I'm sorry." And one by one she gave each reindeer a hug.

"Tomorrow," she said, "we'll go to work in a new way. No yelling, no screaming, and no bossing. I promise. Let me try to help you get free."

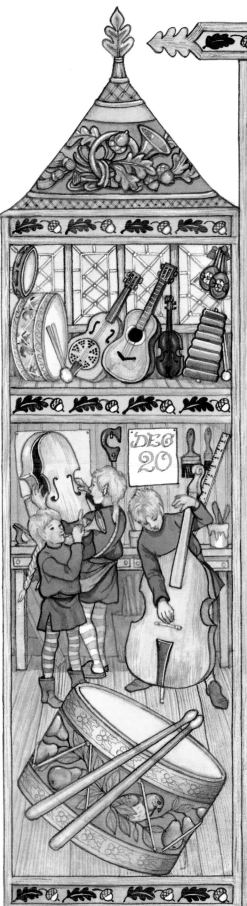

The reindeer listened to this new voice. Heather's eyes sparkled. Crag cracked a reindeer grin. Bramble giggled and Snowball sighed. Tundra laughed and Twilight smiled. The more they laughed, the more they shook and as they shook, their antlers rattled and rubbed.

And before Teeka could do anything, she heard a *spring-spring-sprung* sound. It was the antlers jiggling free.

Quietly, Teeka led the reindeer back to the barn. She sleeked their coats. She gently brushed their ears and combed out their manes. Tundra nuzzled her cheek.

The next day, the reindeer lined up in two lines, ready for the harness, with Twilight and Tundra leading the line. They practiced turning left and they practiced turning right. Teeka directed them softly. Tundra pulled for Twilight. Bramble was gentle to Lichen. Windswept helped Heather, and Snowball nestled against Crag. Together they practiced long and hard.

They didn't notice that it was getting dark, and they almost didn't hear a jingle in the distance. It was Santa standing by the sleigh, piled high with presents and ready to go.

Now the reindeer were ready, too, and Teeka led them to the sleigh. Santa smiled and nodded his thanks. Then he climbed aboard and waved to Teeka who watched as the wild reindeer rose up together and carried the sleigh off into the night.

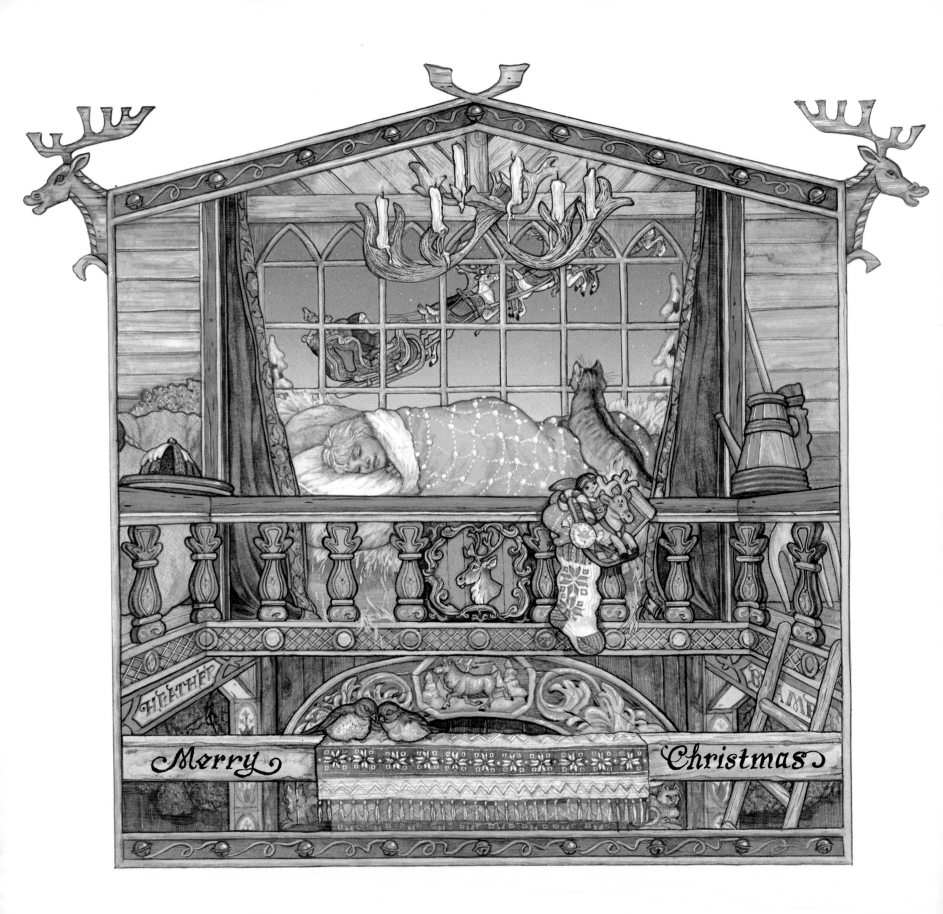